This book belongs to:

Based on the episode "Paddington and the Summer Games" by Adam Redfern

Adapted by Lauren Holowaty

First published in Great Britain by
HarperCollins *Children's Books* in 2021
HarperCollins *Children's Books* is a division of HarperCollins*Publishers* Ltd,
1 London Bridge Street
London SE1 9GF

www.harpercollins.co.uk

HarperCollins*Publishers*
1st Floor, Watermaque Building,
Ringsend Road
Dublin 4, Ireland

1 3 5 7 9 10 8 6 4 2

ISBN: 978-0-00-842084-0

Printed in China

Conditions of Sale

Based on the Paddington novels written and created by Michael Bond

MIX
Paper from
responsible sources
FSC® C007454

FSC
www.fsc.org

FSC is a non-profit international organisation established to promote the
responsible management of the world's forests. Products carrying the FSC
label are independently certified to assure consumers that they come
from forests that are managed to meet the social, economic and
ecological needs of present and future generations.

Find out more about HarperCollins and the environment at
www.harpercollins.co.uk/green

The Adventures of Paddington™

Summer Games

HarperCollins *Children's Books*

Dear Aunt Lucy,

This week I learned that it's not the winning, it's the taking part that counts. And I wasn't the only one who had to learn that lesson . . .

It was a perfect summer's day and Jonathan had just found . . .

"Our box of summer games!" cried Judy, rushing over to see.

"We put them away after Dad got a bit carried away last year," Jonathan told Paddington.

"He *really* likes to win!" said Judy.

Mr Brown came sprinting over.

"Oh no," Jonathan sighed.

"You've found **the summer games!**" said Mr Brown. He picked
up the whistle. "As last year's champion, it's only right I should be ref—"

But before he could finish, Mrs Brown whisked the whistle out of his hand. "*I'll* be referee this time," she said, "just in case."

PFFFTTTT!

"First up, it's the Dizzy Dash!" she announced. "Put your cone on your head, spin round three times, then race to the shed. Ready . . . steady . . ."

PFFFTTTT!

Everyone spun round, counting together, "One, two, three . . .

whoooaaa!"

Paddington, Jonathan and Judy wobbled and bobbled about, bumping into each other and giggling.

Meanwhile, Mr Brown kept his eyes firmly fixed on the finish cone and ran dizzily towards it. "Come on! Come on!" he muttered to himself.

"Winner! Winner! I'm the Dizzy Dash champion!" he shouted, crossing the finish line.

Mrs Brown raised an eyebrow.

"Well, er," mumbled Mr Brown, "we're *all* winners because it's, er, the taking part that counts."

A wobbly Paddington bumped into Mr Brown. "Taking part is certainly lots of fun!"

"The next game is boules," said Mrs Brown. "Closest ball
to the middle of the ring wins."

Judy tossed her ball towards the ring.

"Nice shot!" cried Jonathan. Then he threw his ball next to
hers. **"Yes!"**

Paddington tried to throw his ball but dropped it behind him. He tried once more but dropped it again.

Finally, he turned round and threw it backwards. It landed right in the centre of the ring . . . but bounced out again, stopping beside the other two!

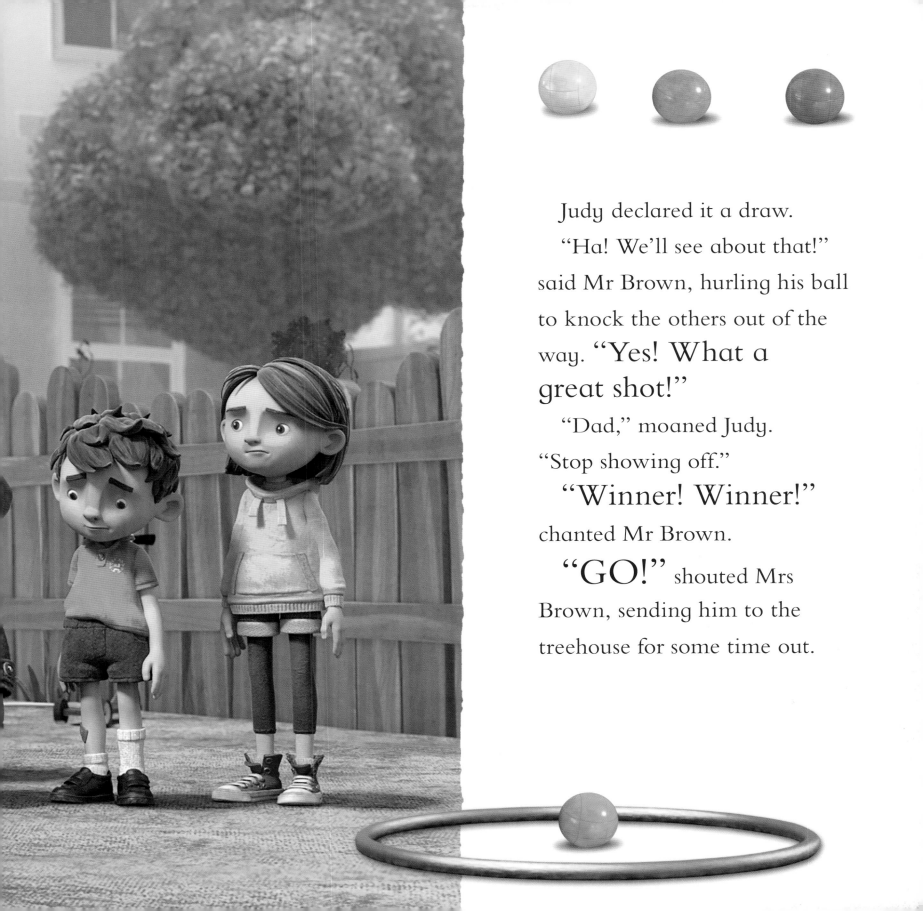

Judy declared it a draw.

"Ha! We'll see about that!" said Mr Brown, hurling his ball to knock the others out of the way. "Yes! What a great shot!"

"Dad," moaned Judy. "Stop showing off."

"Winner! Winner!" chanted Mr Brown.

"GO!" shouted Mrs Brown, sending him to the treehouse for some time out.

Next, it was archery. Mrs Brown, Jonathan and Judy pinged their rubber arrows towards the target.

Boing, boing, boing!

Paddington pulled back his bow and . . .

PER-BOING!

The arrow shot straight up into the sky! Then it plummeted back down into Mr Curry's garden, knocking over the castle he was building for Queen Gnomella. **CRASH!**

"Noooo!" wailed Mr Curry.

Paddington climbed
into the treehouse to see
Mr Brown.

"Mrs Brown says you
can come down if you play
nicely," said Paddington.
"These games are fun."

"No, no. It's *only* fun when
you're winning!" said Mr
Brown. "There's no better
feeling than **winning!**"

Paddington wasn't so sure.
"Oh, I don't know about
that, Mr Brown."

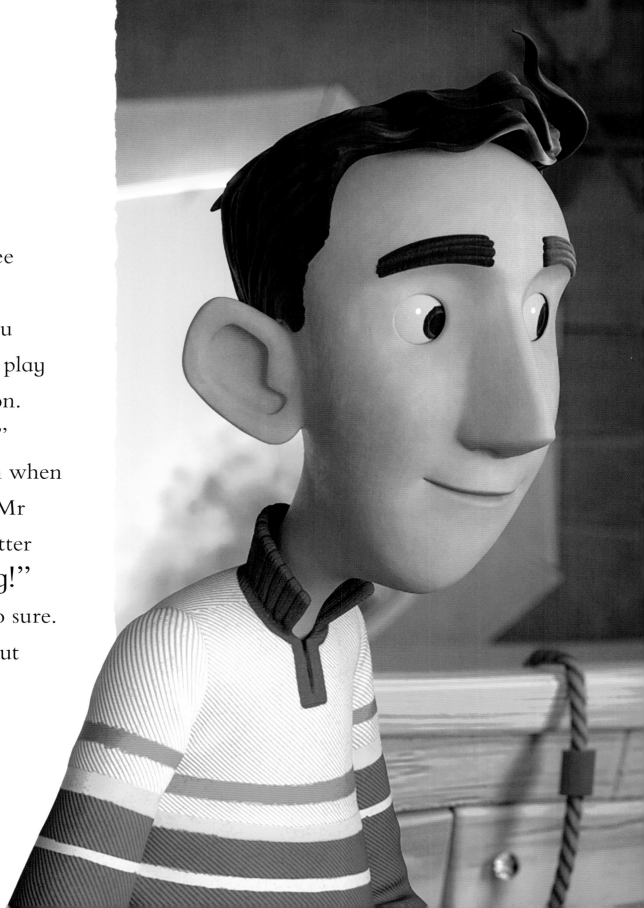

Mrs Brown had set up a badminton net in the garden.

"Right, I'm off to my art class," she said, handing Mr Brown
a racket. "So play *nicely.*"

"Of course," said Mr Brown.

As soon as Mrs Brown had left, Mr Brown shouted, "Game on!"
With a flick of his wrist, Jonathan sent the shuttlecock soaring.
Mr Brown walloped it back. He was determined to win!

SMASH! swooooosh! **SMASH!** swooooosh!

Soon they were playing for the last point in the game . . . Judy leaped into the air and smashed the shuttlecock over the net. It hit the treehouse and landed in the court. "Yessss!" cheered Jonathan and Judy. They'd won!

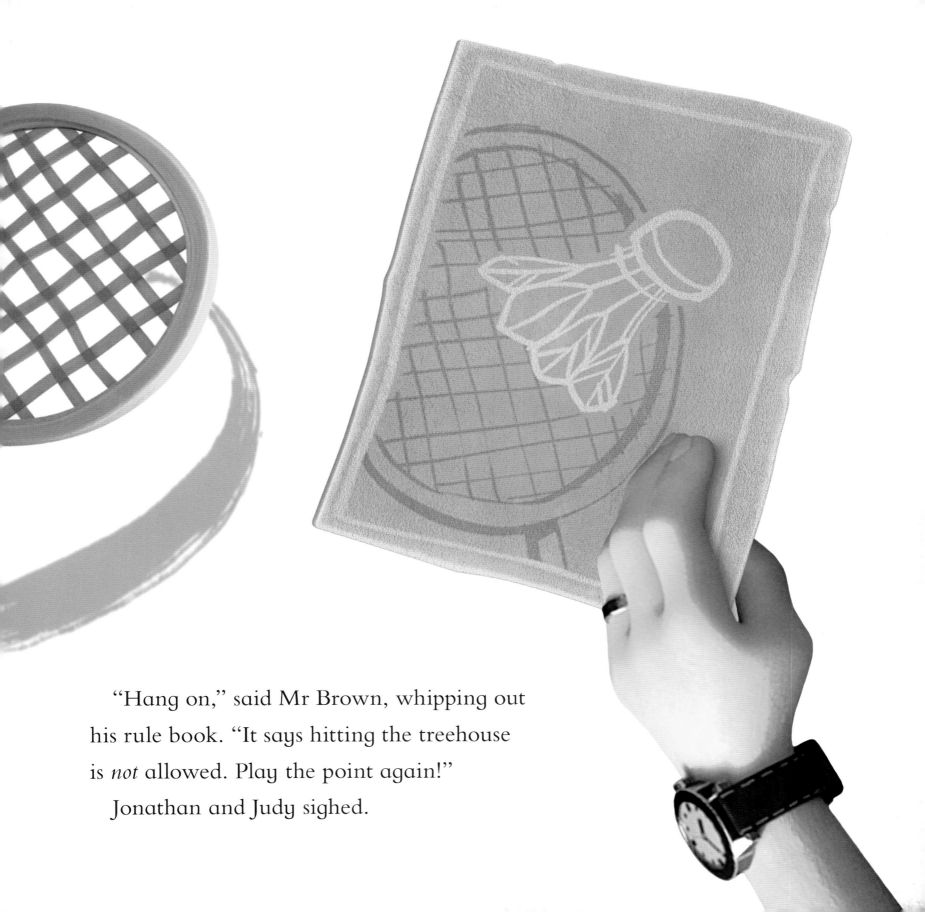

"Hang on," said Mr Brown, whipping out his rule book. "It says hitting the treehouse is *not* allowed. Play the point again!"

Jonathan and Judy sighed.

Judy sent the shuttlecock zooming over to Paddington, but as he went to hit it Mr Brown shouted, "Mine!" He took Paddington's racket and hit the shuttlecock back to win! As he did so, he fell backwards into the fence and knocked over Mr Curry's castle again . . .

CRASH!

Mr Brown leaped up, chanting, "Winner, winner! How does it feel to win, Paddington?"

"*Not* very good, Mr Brown," said Paddington, glumly watching Jonathan and Judy walking away. "You said there's *no better feeling* than winning, but I don't think I've ever felt worse."

Mr Curry stomped into the garden. "Mr Brown, I hope you're happy!" he yelled. "All your winning has done is upset your family, break my fence and ruin Queen Gnomella's castle."

"You're absolutely right," said Mr Brown, hanging his head. "Winning has only made me . . . a bit of a loser." But then he had an idea . . .

Paddington had made Jonathan and Judy sandwiches to cheer them up.

"I'm sorry I got carried away," Mr Brown said. "Can we play just one last game? Please?"

"OK," said Jonathan and Judy reluctantly.

Outside, the whole garden had been turned into a gnome-castle obstacle course.

"Welcome to Queen Gnomella's Royal Race!" said Mr Curry.

"There is just one rule," Mr Brown said. "It's all just for fun!"

"Hooray!" everyone shouted.

The children and Paddington raced round the obstacle
course playing games and collecting castle parts. They had
so much fun working together.

"Finished!" everyone cheered when the castle was rebuilt.
"What a great team!" said Mr Brown.

In the end, Aunt Lucy, we had the most fun as one big team.
And Mr Brown learned that winning doesn't feel good when
it makes others sad. Taking part is the most important thing.
Love from,
Paddington